This is a work of Fiction. Names, Characters, Places, and incidents are products of the Authors imagination or are used fictitiously and are not to be construed as real. Any resemblance to actually events, locales, organizations, or persons, living or dead, is entirely coincidental.

Published by Hush Press

Copyright – 2014 by Fawn Atondo

ISBN 978-0692332146

www.fawnatondo.com

Printed in U.S.A

I'LL BE UNDEAD FOR CHIRSTMAS

Nikki

Nikki wasn't about to waste time with introductions, not when she was 99% sure the person standing outside her door wasn't actually a living person. Call her crazy if you wished, but two hours ago she had seen this same man rip another man's throat open with nothing but his teeth!

And sure, maybe he had inhaled a lot of bath salts or something that morning, but that really didn't explain the glow of his eyes. No, it wasn't the reflection from the street light, not unless it gave off an unholy red sheen, which is what color his eyes had turned. All the sane reasons had run through her head on her return home tonight. In the end, however, the only thing which made any sense at all was she had seen a vampire!

Her heart was pounding like a jackhammer on crack, and all she could think about was the vampire who was hearing this and drooling! Why, oh why hadn't she taken up her mother's offer to come home for the whole month of December? If she had just been a little less dramatic and sucked it up, she wouldn't have been here to run into Mr. Fangs!

"You need to go before I call the cops!" Nikki shouted.

"I am a police officer," a thick voice drawled back.

Braving another peek, she saw the same man outside her door, dressed in faded jeans and a long wool jacket. He didn't look like a cop. Maybe an officer of the Undead Unit, but definitely not one of Boston's finest!

"What kind of officer makes a habit out of stalking women back to their homes?" Nikki demanded.

"The kind who needs to talk to a potential witness?" he offered.

"I didn't witness anything!" Nikki informed him.

"Listen, I am sorry for causing you alarm, but I really am just doing my job." His deep voice was somehow soothing her.

She shook her head trying to keep his dark sexy voice out of it. After all, didn't vampires have powers to control your mind? Nikki knew she wasn't crazy: she *had* seen him bite into another human like he was a chew toy! You couldn't explain that as normal!

"I know what you are, and I am not opening this door!" Nikki said confidently.

"Miss, I don't know what you think you saw, outside of me doing my duty as a police officer, but I can assure you I mean you no harm."

Again his voice made her feel calm, unafraid even.

"Oh really? Is ripping people's throat open with your teeth a thing they teach in Police Academy now?"

"No, but you should open your door. I think you might need medical attention." He sounded worried.

Oh, Nikki didn't doubt if she opened her door she would need medical attention. How did you make it with no throat, after all! Nikki was fighting with her own common sense over what she had really seen. Normally the idea of a vampire lurking outside her home would be a totally crazy thought.

Which left her wondering, was she going mad? Maybe all the drama from the last year had gotten to her? It had been one hellish thing after the other, and her sanity might have checked out for a holiday a little early! She had to figure if the man was truly the undead knocking on her door. How much of an issue did he pose for her, stuck on the other side of it?

Also, if she opened the door and stepped back without inviting him to enter, if all the vampire movies she'd seen and the stories she'd read were true, he couldn't come in. Taking a deep breath and grabbing the fire poker, just in case, Nikki braced herself. Unlatching her deadbolt, she opened her front door.

Holy hell, the man on her doorstep was a looker! Dark brown eyes framed by thick perfect eyebrows. Black hair with only a touch of curl framed a handsome face with a firm jaw. How had she missed he was so damn good-looking?

"See, am I really that horrible?" he asked.

"No, sorry it's been a crazy night," Nikki managed to get out.

"I understand Miss England, but you truly have nothing to fear." His voice was so warming.

"Wait, how do you know my name?" Nikki felt the hairs on her neck starting to stand back up.

"Like I said, I'm an officer. I ran your plates." A slow smile pulled up one side of his full lips.

"Oh… right," she stammered.

"Can I come in?"

"Sure." Nikki answered, still feeling like she was in a bit of a haze.

"Thank you. About what you saw this evening, did you notice the man from the alley in the bar earlier?"

"I think so. Right before I was ready to leave he was leering at me and another girl, but I didn't pay him much attention after that."

Nikki didn't know why she had been so worried about letting this guy in.

"And about your statement about knowing what I am. Did you mean knowing I was a police officer?" His voice was so alluring.

"Um yes, that's what I meant." Wasn't it? She couldn't recall clearly now.

"Good. Now Nikki, I know you have had a rough night and want to get some sleep, but one more thing before I go."

"Yes?" Nikki could feel her whole body stand to attention as he moved closer to her, his mouth mere inches from her own.

"Just one taste." His voice had dropped into a deep rumble, making her insides flutter.

Nikki couldn't find any words, not with all that hotness practically touching her, so she shut her eyes. Leaning in closer, she offered him her mouth. His lips touched hers for one short painful moment before a new kind of pain shattered her haze.

"Shit!" Her voice came out in a hiss.

Damn! She *had* let a vampire into her home! No doubt about it now. Not with his fangs firmly planted in her neck. Nikki could feel herself growing faint, but for the life of her she couldn't fight. She was stuck in his arms like a rag doll as he drained the life from her!

The room was spinning as she felt him ease her down to her sofa, lingering above her. Still handsome, as only one undead could be. His eyes had gone soft as though he was thinking something sweet. If she'd had any strength, she would have laughed at the craziness of the thought!

"I am sorry Nikki, I wish I could have met you under better circumstances, but I couldn't let you go after you saw me. You won't recall my face after this moment." His voice was kind. Only the stain of red on his lips ruined that illusion.

"I don't want to die!" Nikki cried out.

"Hush, you're not going to die, Nikki, just be reborn. On the next full moon you will become like me."

"Like you?" she asked, confused.

"Yes, a vampire."

Vampire! The word rushed through her mind, echoing, till every sense in her body started to tingle. A vampire? No, she couldn't become a vampire!

She wanted to say something. She wanted to demand he fix this. Fix her. But nothing was coming out of her mouth and she was slipping into darkness. Her last thought was of the handsome vampire's lips and how she wished he had just simply kissed her!

The ringing of her phone brought her out of the blackness. She struggled to open her eyes. *Ugh!* Nikki thought as she rolled off her sofa reaching blindly for her cell on the coffee table. Hitting the answer button, she brought it to her ear

"Hello?" Her voice was rough.

"Nikki? You sound like shit!" The rude voice belonged to her co-worker Steven.

"Yeah, it was a crazy night," she grumbled back.

"Sounds like it. Listen, there's breaking news about the Silent Night killer. He's struck again."

This snapped her out of her drunken haze. Nikki couldn't recall much about last night other than staking out the bar in hopes of catching some action; the bar she'd been at was where most of the missing girls ended up being seen last.

Rushing upstairs to her bathroom she looked in the mirror. Her makeup was smeared and her dark hair a mess — clearly a shower wasn't something she'd bothered with after returning home last night and there was no time for one now. Brushing her teeth with one hand while washing her face with the other was a talent all good reporters should possess!

Brushing out her hair she tied it back in a quick ponytail. She was ready to go before she realized she was wearing a cocktail dress! Her jeans from yesterday lay on the bathroom floor along with her light blue sweater. Sniffing to make sure they didn't smell, she quickly redressed.

Nikki didn't drive the speed limit — she was going a constant ten miles over it the whole way through town. Steven had texted her the address of where the crime had taken place. It was located by the docks, and as soon she pulled onto the street she saw why the killer had picked this spot.

It was remote and rundown, giving off a cold feeling even while Boston city lights winked in the background. Parking, she reached for her press pass and slipped it on before seeking out her channel's news van.

Steven was already setting up everything for her. He was doing something in the back of the van and didn't see her approaching. So she gave his shoulder a light tap.

"Nikki! Good God, are you trying to give me a heart attack!" Steven sputtered

"A little jumpy, are we?" she asked with a smile.

"Damn straight! Did you forget there is a dead body somewhere in that building?" he asked with a pointed look.

Nikki didn't answer; she was too busy staring at the old, metal building. No, she hadn't forgotten there was a dead body in there. She knew it would be a young, pretty woman, a girl who had a life up till the sicko took it from her.

Nikki had spent a lot of time trying to figure out who the Silent Night killer was. It was personal to her. He hadn't killed a friend or family member, thank heavens, but he had ruined the spirt of her city for the jolliest part of the year: Christmas.

He didn't just kill one girl, but twelve, and he'd done so every single year for the last three. The police and the FBI hadn't been able to stop him. Being a reporter Nikki had a lot of contacts — she'd met endless amounts of people since she joined KBYO as a reporter. Nikki felt that surely she should be able to dig up some clue to help catch this mad man.

Once upon a time, the twelve days leading up to Christmas had been fun and happy for her, for Boston.

Now they were a nightmare, a countdown of twelve murders! Every young woman in the city had to be on edge; she knew she was.

Steven waved her over. It was time to go on air. Nikki stood in front of the camera taking one last breath. Then she addressed the public.

Sebastian

"Jamison! Come here, you won't believe this!" Dalen called out.

Sebastian pulled the sheet back up over the young woman's face before he went over to the long metal table where his partner was. Joining him, he looked down at a blood-stained bandage. For the first time in three years Sebastian felt a jolt of hope. If this was what they both thought it was, they might actually have something to connect to the Silent Night Killer.

"Do you think it is?" Dalen asked, looking up at him.

"I sure in the hell hope it is!" Sabastian said before he once more looked down at the bandage.

If he was being honest, he already knew this was the killer's blood. He could smell it. Not just the rich smell of blood but the excitement, the joy and the anger that clung to it. This blood was shed in the moment the killer sprung on the young girl. She had fought back, making it all that more enjoyable for the killer. She had left a wound on him, and he was too caught up in this to be careful.

Sebastian had been waiting three long years to get something on the guy; something he could use to hunt him down. This was a break in the case for the department, but it was a bigger break for him. He had spent several human lifetimes working in law enforcement in some shape or form: it was something he liked. Being a vampire was another thing he didn't mind, although that hadn't always been the case. There was a point after his change when he'd really disliked what he was. Vampires had to feed on blood, they couldn't spend a lot of time in the sunlight, and they had to remain unknown to the world. It wasn't until he started working with humans to catch the worst of their kind — the killers, the rapists, the kidnappers — that Sebastian had started to find some peace with being himself.

Now, a hundred and seventy-five years later, he was able to find a balance to being a vampire while keeping his humanity. He didn't want eleven more girls to die this year. He needed to stop this killer before he could hurt anyone else.

Dalen had bagged the bloody bandage. They would send it in to be tested. If they were lucky there might be a match in the system, but at very least they now had DNA. Forensics would finish up at the crime scene before moving the body to the medical examiner's office.

Sebastian wanted to walk around the outside of the building one last time before he went back to the station. It was only a moment after going out the door when he caught two scents. Both of them he knew: one was the killer's, the other's was...

"Nikki." Her name came out in a whisper.

Sebastian looked around and spotted her standing in front of the camera. She wore jeans today instead of the black dress. But she was still beautiful, and the fact he had tasted her made him instantly possessive. He didn't like it — he had never changed a human before — and he didn't like the law which came with a change. The human you made a vampire was yours.

He stayed away from changing for that reason: he didn't want to feel he owned another soul. Even if at this moment he really didn't think he would mind, not one little bit! Seeing her now made it real. He could still hear her heart beating but he knew those were limited beats. In ten days she would be like him.

Mine! he thought before pushing the idea away. No, Nikki, wasn't his, she was no one's. Sebastian knew he would have to find her in ten days to tell her what she had become, but he hadn't planned on seeing her until then.

Nikki had turned and was now staring, her gray-aqua eyes locking onto him. Sebastian knew she liked what she saw, he could taste her desire from here. She was making her way over to him and so was her camera crew.

"Crap!" he muttered.

"Excuse me!" Nikki was calling out to him now.

Sebastian was bracing himself. He didn't like news reporters, even ones as tempting as Nikki. Yet he felt like a jerk for biting her, and why she didn't recall the fact, he sure in the hell did!

"Can I ask you some questions, Officer…" She paused, waiting for a name.

"Jamison," he offered.

"Office Jamison, is it true the Silent Night Killer's first victim for this Christmas season was found today?"

"We can't say for sure, but it looks that way, yes."

"Is there anything at this crime scene that will aid you in finding out who the killer is?"

"There might be, but we don't know it's related at this moment." Damn! He didn't mean to share this much!

"Can you tell me anything more?" Nikki asked, putting the microphone right in his face.

"No, that is all I have." Sebastian turned his back on her and made his way past the yellow tape.

He walked the length of the building following the killer's scent, but it had faded and he couldn't pick it back up. More than a little frustrated, he returned to the station to fill out paperwork. He heard the other detectives turning on the news and realized they would be watching him. Sighing, he tried to focus just on the case and not on the dark-haired long-legged reporter.

It was ten pm and most of the others had gone home. With only eleven more days until Christmas, most had family coming over or were just feeling in the holiday spirit and wanted to be home with loved ones. He didn't have anyone to rush home to, but even if he did he doubted he would be with them, not when his unit was stuck handling the Silent Night killings. The only ones still left by midnight were working on the case.

Time wasn't on their side. They had only hours before the next woman would end up dead. They had officers out patrolling but even they couldn't cover the whole city. Sebastian didn't like to sit around and wait. He wanted to be out searching for the killer. He wanted to save the other girls before they met such a cold ending.

"Hey, you hungry?" Dalen asked.

"Starving," he answered.

"I'll go pick us up some sandwiches from Tom's Deli," Dalen said putting his jacket on.

"Thanks," Sebastian answered absent-mindedly.

He was starving, but not for a sandwich. He needed blood at least once a week to keep himself sane: vampires didn't do well mentally if they skipped a meal. Sebastian wasn't nearing the tipping point yet, however, he didn't like to push out feedings.

Dalen return half an hour later with their food. Sebastian ate it without even tasting it. His focus was wholeheartedly on the case. Which ended up dragging on into the early morning hours.

It was seven thirty am when the call came in.

Another body had been found. This time in an upper-crust neighborhood park. The girl was just like the others: naked with strangulation marks on her neck. Posed in a Sleeping Beauty position, hands folded over each other resting on her chest.

For a split second he had thought it could be Nikki — the girl looked very much like her — but once he got closer, he saw the girl's face was more angular and not a soft oval. Sebastian leaned down close and inhaled the smells.

The metallic earthy smell of blood mixed in with the killer's scent. This time the scent was strong. Sebastian followed it across the park. He ended up walking for thirty minutes till he came to an older subdivision built in the late fifties. The scent lead to a brown-bricked home on the end of the street.

He wanted to kick in the door and confront whoever he found inside, but he knew Dalen would ask how he'd found the house, and so would his superiors. So he told a little white lie over his radio, and within five minutes cop cars filled the street in front of the house.

"Definitely more careless than in previous years," Dalen said with a shake of his head.

"Lucky for us," Sebastian stated before moving up to the front door.

In a loud voice, which carried down the street, he informed anyone who may be inside exactly who was outside their door.

"Boston Police! Open up!"

He didn't wait for anyone to reply or open the door. He kicked it hard, sending wood splinters everywhere.

Police officers flooded inside and, after a few moments, it was clear no one was there. Just as quickly, though, they knew without doubt the Silent Night Killer had been calling this home! Above the stone fireplace were twelve stockings.

The first two bore the names of the two recent victims. Chillingly, the other ten also had names on them. On the eleventh stocking was a name that gave Sebastian pause. There, in blood-red thread, was 'Nikki England'.

He planned to kill her one day before the full moon on Christmas Eve, meaning if the killer got his hands on Nikki, she wouldn't be coming back. She wouldn't be a new member of the undead — she would simply just be dead.

Sebastian knew he wouldn't be waiting to see Nikki again. He would have to become her shadow because he damn well wasn't going to let any harm come to her.

"We are going to have to find all these women, and sooner rather than later!" Dalen was saying.

"I know Nikki England."

"You know her? How?" Dalen asked.

"Well, I know *of* her. She's a reporter. She was at the last crime scene."

"You going to be the one to break the news to her?"

Oh, he sure was! And not just the fact she was a target of a serial killer, he would also have to tell her that in nine days and elven hours, she would be reborn a member of the undead! Sebastian didn't see this going down any other way but bad.

Nikki

It had been a crazy day! Nikki's mind couldn't take any more new developments on the Silent Night Killer. After the body of the second victim of the year was found this morning, another discovery hit the news waves like a category five hurricane!

Her crew had barely started setting up at the crime scene when word broke that the killer's house had been found. A rumor started spreading about finding the names of the two girls who had already been killed, and of the other ten who would be.

It was more than a little creepy to think the killer had made stockings for all his victims. If this was even true — Nikki knew how badly the news could get facts wrong!

After finally finishing her shift and being able to get a shower, she ordered pizza. Sitting in front of her TV, she watched as stories begun to pour in about the Silent Night Killer and his house of horrors. Nikki was sure most of Boston was glued to news channels as well. She was waiting on the elven o'clock bulletin when her doorbell rang.

This did more than make her hair stand up on end on the back of her neck. She was a logical person most of the time, but with all this talk of murder she was feeling a little jumpy. Nikki went for her fire poker, only to find it missing.

"What the hell?" she whispered.

She stared toward the door to peek out her window, and saw the poker behind her sofa. With a double take, Nikki reached down and picked it up. Feeling a little more confident now she peeped out the door to see a Boston policeman on her doorstep. She couldn't see his face but she saw his chest well enough.

Opening the door she was a little shocked to see it was Officer Jamison! A warning bell went off in the back of her mind with a sense of déjà vu.

"Can I help you, Officer Jamison?"

"I need you to come down to the station with me." His voice was deep and all male.

"Why? Did I do something wrong?" Nikki was pretty sure she hadn't broken any laws lately.

"No nothing like that, we just need to talk to you," he assured her.

Nikki didn't know what was going on but she was smart enough to do as the officer wanted. Or should she say 'detective'? She had done some digging on Officer Jamison after their interview and she learned he was no mere Boston policeman.

"Let me grab my purse first."

Nikki quickly locked up the house and followed Jamison out to his car.

It was an awkward silence as they sat side by side on their way to the station. Nikki kept sneaking looks when she was sure he wasn't looking her way. He really was handsome which was making this whole ride a degree more uncomfortable.

It took them a little over twenty minutes to reach the station. In all that time neither of them so much as smiled at the other. Nikki was in the process of removing her seatbelt when Jamison reached across her to relatch it.

"Stay here, I'll be right back."

Getting out, he locked the squad car. Which Nikki found odd, but she did as she was told. He had a good reason, surely. Five minutes later he returned. Getting in, he started the car, and then pulled back into traffic.

"I thought you had questions for me?" Nikki asked.

"I do."

"Then where are we going?" Nikki wondered as they headed toward Beacon Hill.

"I'm taking you some place safe."

"Where?"

"My house."

Nikki felt her jaw drop a little as she looked over at him. He was still staring straight ahead and not paying her any attention.

"Is that professional, officer?" Nikki demanded. It didn't feel like it should be.

"I am more than qualified to keep you safe, Miss England," he told her with a hint of amusement in his voice.

Nikki couldn't argue the point. She knew from her research he was. Still, she didn't like the warning bells her mind kept sending her body! Something more was at play here.

"Why your house and not mine?"

"Because it's highly likely the killer knows your house by now. You're not safe there." His response was logical.

"Why would the killer be at my house?"

"Because, Nikki, you're on his list."

Nikki was stunned for a moment. If the killer really was after her then how long would she have to shack up with Officer Jamison?

"And how long do you plan to keep me at your house?"

"As long as it takes."

"I have a job, you know. I can't lock myself up while you guys try and catch a man you haven't been able to find in three years!"

"I understand you have a job to do, Miss England, and you may keep working as long as it is safe to."

"And if you think it isn't?"

"Then you will stay locked up." His tone was matter-of-fact.

Nikki let out a little huff as she crossed her arms over her chest. She didn't like being told what to do, even by someone who was trying to keep her safe!

"I don't even have my clothes, my toothbrush… anything!"

"Once I have you safely back at my house, I will have an officer go to your home and get your stuff."

"How will he know what to pack? Can't I go with him?" Nikki asked.

"No. He will bring all your things… you will have what you need, I promise."

He turned to look at her now.

"Nikki?" his tone was soft almost seductive.

"Yeah?"

"It's okay to be afraid, but I will keep you safe." His eyes reflected the truth of his words.

"Jamison?"

"Yes?"

"I'm not afraid. I'm pissed!" Nikki gave him a hard glare before turning herself away from him.

His house was a bloody mansion! It was a dark-grey smooth-stone three-story house. It had a dark iron gate which they were driving through now. Nikki couldn't look away from the place: it was lovely in a dark, silent-movie kind of a way. It was like stepping back a few centuries.

Jamison parked the car in front of the cobble-stoned walkway. Nikki didn't know detectives made this much money! Still busy looking at the huge house, she didn't even notice Jamison had come around and opened the door for her.

"The inside is even better." His words pulled her from her gawking.

"Sorry, but this place is huge! I never would have thought a police officer could afford such a house!"

"They don't usually, but my family came from money. They're gone and I got the estate."

"Oh," she said with a flush to her face.

He was right: the inside *was* even grander. A sweeping staircase and wide marble floors greeted her when she stepped inside. To the left was a set of white plush chairs facing the floor-to-ceiling window. It looked like a sitting room. Nikki followed him past this and down a long hallway which opened up into a living room so large it had four sofas artfully placed in the mix with more chairs, a few end tables and one large glass coffee table. A huge flat-screen TV took up one wall, but otherwise the walls were bare of photos or artwork.

"This place is really something," Nikki whispered as she walked around the room.

"It can be a bit overwhelming but you will quickly find it's rather cozy." He had a shadow of a smile on his lips.

"Right," she said with a roll of her eyes.

"I am going to make a call to have someone come get your keys so they can bring your stuff over. It might not be till morning, however," he told her as he put his cell to his ear.

"Okay."

Nikki walked the length of the massive room, finding yet another hallway which seemed to lead to the second floor. While the reporter in her wanted to be nosey and poke around, the guest part of her knew it would be impolite to impose before her host gave her the green light.

"Someone will be by in the morning." He was standing behind her.

Turning, Nikki found herself looking at a bare-chested Officer Jamison. This made it hard for her to focus on what else he was saying. She couldn't peel her eyes from his chest, although she managed in fact to steal a glance even lower to his perfectly flat, well-defined stomach.

"Miss England?" he asked, a little on the loud side.

Startled out of her eye-sexting, she looked up to find his eyes almost glowing. Yes, his dark gaze seemed to be burning with a yellow fire.

"Yeah?"

"I was just asking if you wanted to borrow a T-shirt for tonight." His voice was rich as honey and twice as sweet.

"Yes, thank you." Nikki felt her stomach flutter and knew if he didn't find a shirt for himself as well, she couldn't be held responsible for what she did!

"Come on, I'll show your to your room and find you something to sleep in."

He turned around, giving her all the time in the world to take him in from behind. He had a wide back which led to a nice ass, and she would bet all her life savings his legs were just as toned and perfect as the rest of him. He made her feel like she needed to work on her own physique!

Nikki didn't even give the second floor a fleeting glance when she first got there, too lost in naughty thoughts to care about the décor. He showed her to a room all done in white, from the walls to the bedding. It was more tight and neat than a hotel!

"You have a knack for decorating, Jamison." She gave him a smile when he looked back at her.

"Sebastian."

"Excuse me?"

"My name is Sebastian. Since we are going to be sharing a home for a while, I think we can go by first names, don't you... Nikki?"

The way he said her name made her insides do the happy dance. He was a sexy man, a man she badly wanted to see naked... in her bed... for a long... long... time...

Nikki forced herself to stop thinking about him like that.

"Jam— Sebastian, about that night shirt?" Nikki made sure to keep eye contact this time, hoping it would keep her mind out of the gutter.

"I'll be right back."

Once he left, she went to the bed. Laying down on it, closing her eyes.

Okay Nikki, keep it PG.... keep it PG. It didn't stick. Within a few moments she was lost in a daydream... one which had Sebastian all over her, she all over him. The heat spread through her body as she imagined what his hands would feel like, his lips.

Oh, she should be worried a serial killer had marked her as his victim. She should be worried about how her life was about to get turned upside down, about how she should keep a good twenty feet between her and Officer Jamison, but none of it seemed to matter.

Sebastian

He stopped outside Nikki's bedroom. He was about to just walk in, but the emotion he picked up, her thoughts, stopped him in his tracks. He held one of his shirts in his hands with a death grip. The taste of desire was so strong he closed his eyes, drinking it in. Feeling what she was feeling.

He hadn't missed the lust in her stare when he came back into the living room, minus his shirt. Still, it hadn't prepared him for what she was feeling right now. He knew, without a doubt, if he were to walk in there, push her back on the bed, peel her clothes off and fuck her senseless, she wouldn't object.

If he hadn't bitten her then he would already be in there, in her. The issue was he had, so if he also took her to his bed he wouldn't be able to turn away and not claim her. Fighting the possessive feelings he was having now was bad enough, but if he gave into his need to take her, then that would be it!

He blocked himself off from feeling what she was and forced the door open. She lay on the bed, her eyes closed, her dark hair spread out over the white sheets, making it even darker. He saw the smooth flatness of her belly.

Lord, have mercy! How could he fight this if she was going to make it so damn easy to take her?

Sebastian cleared his throat. Nikki shot up faster than a bullet, her eyes wide with a slight touch of guilt mixed with desire. They were more aqua than grey in her lust. Her mouth was lush full, maybe the fullest pair of lips he had ever seen.

"I..." She stopped, looking down at the shirt he still had a death grip on.

He quickly loosened his grip before holding it out to her. She got up deliberately, taking painfully slow steps toward him.

"Sebastian." She said his name with all the tenderness and passion a lover would. He was on a fast track to giving in to his nature, to the darker side of himself, the part which was more vampire then human.

"Nikki, I can't do this..." was all he got out before she pulled the shirt from his hands.

She took two steps back before reaching for the buttons on her jeans. With a flick of her wrist she had them undone. He could have turned away and walked back out the door, but he didn't. Instead, he watched with a growing sense of triumph.

Nikki kicked her jeans away before pulling her shirt off over her head. No bra. His eyes locked on to her breasts. Perfect, full, with taut pink nipples. He licked his lips. He could feel his teeth lengthen as he watched her.

Nikki's own eyes danced with fire as she pulled his T-shirt on. It fell to her thighs, but seeing her in his T-shirt was more arousing to him than if she were standing there naked. He let out a soft groan and took a step toward her.

She took another step back before holding her hand up. He stopped on seeing this, a bit confused as he tried to understand what was happing through the thick fog of sexual tension.

"Sebastian, this is too complicated. You're right, we can't." Her voice shook a little as she turned around and got into the bed, pulling the blankets up to her chin.

He stood there like a fool, watching her for a few moments, before he was able to walk away. Every step was painful, for his teeth weren't the only thing that had grown with her little show back there.

Closing her door with a defining click, he headed up one story to the third floor, which was where his gym was. He needed to punch something till the emotion inside him was back under control. One thing was clear now: Nikki England was a dangerous woman, and he couldn't risk telling her what she was going to become before her turning.

Vampires tended to be ruled by their instincts, the strongest of those being ownership of what they deemed theirs. They didn't waver in their feelings: if they felt for someone or something then they would protect it.

If it was a mate or a member of their coven it was even stronger. Those who didn't keep in check their human side became more aggressive in this area. While Sebastian held on to his humanity, he still had the urges of a vampire. Mainly those of blood and claiming rights of the bite.

He hadn't thought the turning would turn out be this strong. He'd heard stories, of course, but having never turned anyone before, he didn't know just how powerful it truly was. Not all who were changed ended up being a mate. Most turns were looked after, educated in the ways of the vampire and sent out on their way.

Other times... well, other times a bite led to a connection — to a linking of souls which naturally led to a mate. A mate was claimed by the vampire through the act of sex, and afterwards, the one claimed was theirs for life. It was a little barbaric to Sebastian: he didn't want to take away the willpower of someone he'd been forced to change!

Even if this one was making it damn hard not too...

And, if he was completely honest with himself, he knew the reason he didn't want to tell Nikki what she was about to become: he hadn't fully made up his mind not to sleep with her, to make her his. It wasn't something he liked, the vampire side ruling over his humanity.

He had worked hard to perfect the balance he had. To only drink from the sinners, to protect the innocent, and, no matter how tempting his sexy reporter might be, she was still among the innocent and didn't deserve to be forced into a union she couldn't get out of.... Ever.

Sebastian spent the night watching Nikki's house. He was hoping the killer would show up. He would have to know the police would be moving the girls he had named. There was always the chance he would find new victims, but Sebastian didn't think so. The Silent Night Killer spent most the year picking his girls before he moved into kill them.

He arrived back home in the early hours of dawn. He checked in on Nikki, who was sleeping soundly, so he went downstairs to catch a few hours of sleep. The day was always more restful for a vampire's sleep, but it didn't keep them locked indoors. The older they got, the less the daylight would bother them. They would always need to wear sunglasses if they wished to avoid a headache but they didn't fear it, like so many humans imagined. The only fact the common myths had right about a vampire was they drank blood. Vampires didn't need only blood, nor all that often. Feeding once or twice a week sufficed.

There would always be an evil element among his kind, those who murdered for pure enjoyment, but they weren't allowed to get out of control. If a vampire became too much of a risk there would always be another willing to take them out.

Sebastian wasn't about to take away Nikki's free will just because her mind had been strong enough to fight most of his compulsions. He was going to have to pull out the professional card with her and keep it firmly between them. Giving into their mutual attraction, they would both be losing something.

He heard her moving around upstairs. She was going to be hungry so he set out making breakfast. Eggs and bacon. Sebastian nearly had it ready when she finally made her way down stairs.

"That smells wonderful," she said with a small smile.

He could see the look of embarrassment in her eyes.

"I make a mean breakfast," he informed her.

"Listen, about last night... I'm not sure what came over me. I plead insanity and I am sorry for acting like a hussy." Her face was bright red by the time she finished.

"I like you, Nikki. Let's face it, I think you're sexy as hell but we can't... you know... You're under my protection. I'm an officer of the law and I can't sleep with someone I'm charged with keeping safe."

He held her gaze for a moment before returning to flipping the eggs.

"I get it."

"Good, now let's forget it." He gave her a half smile as he slid a plate to her.

They ate without much chatter. She asked about work a few times, and he agreed that once she'd got her stuff, he would take her down to the station to check in with them. They now had nine days till Christmas. If they reached all the remaining marked girls in time, they wouldn't be getting another call about a body.

Nikki seemed eager to get to work. She was more reserved today than any of the times he had met her before, even the night she discovered what he was. He didn't like the change, but he knew they needed this.

The news was still swarming about the discovery of the Silent Night Killer's home. And Nikki's station wanted her on-scene. Sebastian wasn't overly worried about her, not with all the news crews and cops still around, but he wouldn't let her go alone.

Nikki asked if she could ride with her cameraman, and Sebastian agreed. It didn't stop him from tailgating the news van all the way to the crime scene, though. Nikki shot him a look of annoyance when they got there but didn't say a word to him.

She was soon so busy giving her report and working with her crew and he was forgotten. Sebastian took the time to watch the people around her. He got a call from Dalen with an update about the other women.

All but two of them had been found and moved. It was a race to find the last two, and Sebastian prayed they found them before the killer did.

Thankfully the media hadn't learned any of the names on the list, or if there even was one for sure. It would help keep the woman out of the limelight and make it a whole lot easier to keep them safe. Of course, his charge would have to be part of the media circus!

It was likely this reason the killer had picked her. She was his type, and he got to see her face daily on the news. If he killed her it would make him even more notorious, and he would love that. The profile on this guy had him pinpointed as the kind you didn't want to run into, even in the light of day.

Nikki had gone into the news van and seemed to be taking for ever to come out. Even her camera guy seemed worried. Sighing, Sebastian made his way over to the van. He asked the skinny blond-haired man what was wrong.

"I would have to guess, based on the thumping noises, she's having a seizure or something!" he grumbled as another loud bang came from inside. "Watch it, Nikki! That stuff isn't cheap, for Chrissakes!" the cameraman pleaded.

"Nothing's… broken… yet." Nikki sounded out of breath.

"Nikki?" Sebastian called her name.

"Go away, Jamison!" she barked.

Another loud thump came, followed by a groan. Sebastian had a sinking feeling he knew what was happening. If he was right, Nikki was feeling the first effects of the change. Thankfully she was out of sight.

Sebastian prayed Nikki wasn't causing too much unexplainable damage to the inside of the van! If this was a sign of things to come, it was about to get tricky.

Nikki

The spasms kept coming, rocking her body like an aftershock. Nikki watched helplessly as her muscles twitched, sending her right arm smashing down into some equipment. Flinching, she hoped she hadn't broken it.

She didn't get time to worry about it because another wave hit her, sending her whole body into the opposite side of the news van. Cursing, she pushed herself back to her feet before dropping to the floor. Wrapping her arms around herself, she tried to hold the spasms back.

Just as quickly as they had started, they passed, leaving her breathless and drained. Nikki could hear someone knocking on the van doors, and she hoped it was Steven. The muscles in her legs screamed in protest at being stretched but she forced herself to stand and open the door.

Sebastian was waiting for her, his face pinched in worry. Nikki gave him a smile before stepping out. Her legs crumpled, pitching her forward right into Sebastian's arms.

"Sorry."

"Are you okay?" He still held her, his arms locked around her.

"I think so."

"What was going on in there?" Sebastian's breath warmed the side of her face.

"A bee." It was a horrible lie and she knew it.

"A bee?" He didn't sound convinced.

"Yes, you know, black and yellow with a stinger? A bee!" she snapped as she pushed herself off his chest.

"I know what a bee is, Nikki, but it's thirty-two degrees out. Not exactly bee-friendly weather," Sebastian pointed out.

"Clearly this bee didn't get the memo!"

"Um-hum." He shot her a look with those dark brown eyes.

"I'm done for the moment, if you're ready to leave," Nikki said, changing the subject.

"I was thinking we could make a pit stop at the station on the way back?"

"Sure, as long as you don't leave me in the car this time."

Once more Sebastian didn't say anything. He only gave her a long, hard look before turning away.

At the station he finally spoke.

"Nikki, you are going to talk with a few officers. I'll be there, but since you're staying with me I won't be the one asking questions."

His words didn't matter. Not with his hand resting softly on her face.

Caught off-guard by this, she simply stared at him, trying to figure out what it was about him which pulled her in. It was not just his looks, although he was handsome, and hauntingly so. No, there was this vibe which came off him that made her want to get closer — demanded it, even.

"Are you ready?" His voice gave away, ever so slightly, he too felt something.

"Yes."

And both of them seemed to catch she wasn't talking about the interview.

Sebastian led her through the building to a long hallway where she shook hands with two very tall, lanky detectives. They could have been twins, except the female detective had jet black hair and the male's was so light, it could have passed for white.

Both were friendly but to the point. After nearly an hour of what Nikki was sure had to be pointless questions, they allowed her to go.

Nikki didn't want to spend another sexually-charged night with Sebastian, not when it was clear he didn't want to mix work and pleasure. On the other hand, she was very sure that if she set out to seduce him… well, it wouldn't be hard.

He seemed tense as they pulled up to his home. It was like he was making a point of avoiding getting close to her. It was turning into something painful to watch. Nikki had been delighted to learn her things were now here, and took as much time as she could putting them away in the bedroom.

Still, a girl could only spend so long unpacking before she got bored! The fitted cotton shorts and low plunging t-shirt she put on were done with one thing in mind. Seducing Sebastian!

It was a little shameful to be trying to force his hand, or rather his hands onto her own person, as the case may be, but Nikki couldn't help but give into the natural sexual urge to seduce. Sebastian was making dinner — something with spice, judging from what she was smelling.

The marble kitchen was lit with a soft overhead glow. Sebastian stood at the stove in a pair of snug jeans and a white tank top. His dark hair a mix between bedroom hair and edgy CEO. Licking her lips while suppressing a sigh, she walked right up to him.

Close enough. Her hips brushed his thighs. There was no way to ignore her if she was this much in his space. His gaze ran up from her breasts to her eyes, where they locked, sending a spark of lust through her whole body.

"You have no idea who you're flirting with," his voice was hard.

The way his voice sounded with a touch of danger made the little hairs on her arms stick up. Nikki looked down before looking back into his eyes, and what she saw there was clear: sexual desire and ownership.

"I am well aware you want me and that you're a little controlling, Sebastian... but I don't care!"

Sebastian let out a soft groan before he turned his whole body so it pressed into hers. He wrapped one arm around her waist, and the other he slipped around the back of her neck.

"A little controlling, Nikki? With you there is no 'little'!" Then he bent his head and ravished her mouth.

This was a kiss unlike any other she had ever shared. It was intense, possessive and sexual. It melted her insides, curled her toes. Nikki could now say she had felt fireworks from a kiss! Running her hands over all those lean hard lines in his arms and chest was just icing on the cake.

Sebastian broke the kiss, much to her dismay, but when he scooped her up in his arms all was forgiven. He didn't make it to the bedroom or even the living room, but stopped in the sitting room, dropping her on the small sofa by the window.

"If I do this, if I take you, there is no going back." He forced her chin up so her eyes met his.

"I understand." And she thought she did: if they did this, there was no going back to witness and protector.

He sighed long and hard, his face twisted in a mix of passion and control before he shook his dark head.

"No, I really don't think you do." His words were soft and lost in the crook of her neck.

Sebastian kissed her neck, teasing with his lips and teeth before locking onto her ear, sending a rush of heat right to her core. One hand worked to remove her shorts, and there was a sound of approval at finding no undies to block his fingers from her heat.

His fingers pushed farther inside her, drawing a low gasp from her lips, her own fingers digging deeper into his shoulder blades. She had never wanted something so much in all her life. In this moment she didn't want to think about regrets or what tomorrow would mean for them both.

Nikki wrapped her hands around the hem of his tank and pulled it up. Once it was free she pushed him back till she was the one on top. Leaning forward, she dipped her head down to taste the hard lean planes of his chest. Lower, till she was licking the flat of his stomach. He sucked in a breath before his hands became buried in her hair.

With a wicked smile on her lips, she nipped along the edge of his jeans right on his hip bones, which earned her a hard tug to the fistful of hair he was holding. She was working the zipper on his pants when the loud dinging of the doorbell shattered their lustful haze.

With a long stream of cuss words, Sebastian sat up, sending her sliding down him and onto the sofa. With a look of disappointment sent her way he went to answer his door. Now Nikki let go a few choice words of her own!

Pulling back on her shorts, she tiptoed toward the foyer. A man dressed in Boston PD uninform was standing just inside the doorway talking with Sebastian. They were whispering, allowing her to only catch a few words.

Nikki heard enough to know they had found another body. All thoughts of crazy sexual fulfillment melted away. Sebastian ended with the promise of going down to the station. Shutting the door, he turned, his eyes going right to hers.

"They found the body of the next victim in order of the stockings." His voice was flat.

"I thought all of us were being protected?" Nikki heard the panic in her words.

"They are," he said quietly.

The look on his face said more. He wasn't happy, and he had no idea how to stop this monster, which shook his confidence. Somehow the Silent Night Killer was able to snatch the women right from under their noses. Nikki knew on her own face was a question — one neither wanted to answer. How safe was she really?

SEBASTIAN

There were only eight days to go until Christmas and the city was blanketed in white snow and holiday lights. It looked picture perfect, yet under the sweet wrapped-up appearance of cheer, the people of Boston where on edge.

Sebastian didn't have to give Nikki a reason why she was coming with them. It was all too clear she was frightened. It had been hours since he had left her at his desk. He was in the large room in the back that served as their conference room.

Angie Gates had been kidnapped right out of the house Witness Protection had set her up in. The policeman assigned to watch her was found with his throat slit. They were in a race against time to keep the media from learning all the dirty details.

And a leader among them sat at his desk. She wouldn't hold back from sharing what she had learned. Not when it was her job. Reporters — the good ones — have a natural need to tell the truth behind newsworthy events.

Sebastian's boss was having a hard time coming to terms that a woman was murdered while under their watch. And they had just learned another one of the woman was missing: the officer protecting her had not checked in.

Sebastian didn't have a good feeling. Sitting around the table, Boston's finest waited for the officer they'd dispatched to check on Lisa Mack to update them.

Forensics had reported back about the bandage, but the perp wasn't in the system. Sebastian wasn't all that surprised to learn no name or identity had been found at the rental property the murderer had been squatting in.

The phone on the table rang and the captain answered it before the first ring could finish. His face pinched up, causing the lines on his face to deepen.

"Son of a bitch!" the captain muttered before slamming the phone down. "She's gone. The officer was found dead in his car, just like Robertson," he said, running his large hand down his face. "We're going to be getting a call about another body soon. The media is going to send panic through the city once they learn the women we thought safe are still being taken!"

"There isn't much we can do about that, Cap, but we can do something about the remaining woman," Dalen said.

"We need to move the others, and quick," Sebastian agreed.

"So we move them, but then what? Does this keep the lunatic from finding them?" the captain demanded.

"We'll catch him," Sebastian assured him.

"It's only a little more than a week before Christmas, for godssakes! Who is going to be singing fucking 'Jingle Bells' while women are getting murdered, one by one, like some sick version of a gift offering?"

Once more their captain was losing it.

"Go home, Cap, see the missus and the grandkids. Leave the dirty work to me and Jamison for now. We will catch this SOB," Dalen told him.

Sebastian walked the captain out and checked on Nikki. She was passed out, her head on the desk. He threw his jacket over her shoulders before going back to the conference room. He didn't like the feelings he was getting. The Silent Night Killer was turning out to be a cunning murderer, yet nothing about his ability screamed typical human psychopath. No, his gut was telling him there was something more to this killer — something supernatural.

"This isn't looking good, my friend," Dalen sighed, when Sebastian came back in.

"I know, there is something not adding up here."

"You got that right, Jamison. Where do we move the others to?"

"We move them out of State."

Dalen looked shocked but recovered quickly before he let out a long, low whistle and picked up the phone.

"The Feds aren't going to like the cost in relocating all of them out of State. What about your girl?"

"Nikki stays with me, just move the others," Sebastian barked out before leaving his partner to the task.

Nikki was no longer sleeping when he came back. She was very much awake and on the phone. His stomach tightened, wondering if she was already filling her station in.

He moved forward till he was standing right next to her. She wasn't talking to anyone at work.

"Yes, Mom, I'm fine. I'm sorry I haven't called in a few days but it's been crazy over here." Her voice sounded sleepy. "Yes, I'm busy because of the killings, Mom. But I'm safe so don't worry about me. I love you too."

She hung up but he didn't miss the tears in her eyes.

"Your mom checking in?" he asked gently.

"Yeah, she worries. I couldn't tell her I've been chosen as one of the Silent Night Killer's victims." She shook her head at the thought.

"Good. Because she would be worried for no reason: I'm not going to let him touch you," Sebastian told her.

"I know." She didn't sound like she fully believed that, though.

"We only have to keep you safe seven more days," he said, tilting her chin up.

"Seven more days? Christmas isn't for eight!"

"You only need to make it past your chosen day."

"And then what? He takes the year off?" she said with a huff.

"No, after that he won't be able to hurt you," Sebastian said firmly.

Nikki gave him a funny look as though she was trying to understand what he meant. He decided it was time to change the topic.

"We are going to go do something festive." He gave her a bright smile.

"What?" she asked, clearly taken aback by the turnaround in the conversation.

"It's nearly Christmas so you should be having some holiday cheer." He took her hand, pulling her along after him.

Outside the snow was falling softly, and he knew just where to take her. Downtown was a cute little café which had the best eggnog in the city. He would get her insides warm and her spirts up with its charming decor of green, red and silver.

Nikki broke out in a slow smile when they pulled up outside. She turned quickly, placing a sweet kiss to his cheek before opening the car door. He touched the place her lips had just been. It wasn't a kiss meant to undo him, but the innocent, easy, caring way she gave it stunned him, even as it warmed his undead heart.

Inside they sat by the frost-covered window full of twinkling white lights with candy canes and Christmas trees painted on the glass. She talked about her childhood and her family. He listened and offered a few stories from his past.

It was then, in this still winter moment, a girl stole his heart. She did it with a pure easy smile, which showed the sweetness of her soul, the fire in her blood. Nikki England wasn't just a woman he found sexy, a woman he wanted to bed. She was a woman he wanted to share a life with. To fill a house with joy, and lots more simple, easy moments like this.

Sebastian froze, his heart barely beating, as he realized he would never be able to let Nikki go. However, he would never seal her to him before knowing she felt the same as he did, without the power of him being her maker.

"Are you okay?" she asked, her forehead bunched up in worry.

"Never better," he answered with a knowing look.

Blushing, she pushed her hair from her face and went on with another of her stories. He listened to her talk for hours, happy to learn all about her.

"Sebastian, about earlier tonight, I want you to know I do want to be with you like that. However, I wouldn't want to force you to cross any lines you are not willing to. I guess what I'm trying to say is I can wait till this is done before we... you know." She winked.

"I want you. And I want you to understand I am not just willing to have you for a night, I want to have you for a lifetime." *Many lifetimes*, he added silently.

Nikki's eyes got big as she looked at him, trying to figure out what he meant by this. Surely he must be mad to feel this way so soon.

"I don't even know what to say to that. How can you feel this way after a few days?"

"I figured you would think I'm crazy, and I could be, but only for you. We share something, can't you feel it?" he wanted to know.

"I don't deny we have something, some connection I can't understand, but a lifetime is like saying 'I love you, I want to marry you'! Can I accept that after two days? No, I can't, Sebastian. It doesn't make any sense!"

"Did I pop the question?" he asked in mock horror.

"Well, no, but..."

"No. All I said was a lifetime. I want you, Nikki, but if you are not there yet that's fine. I didn't say you had to be. Hell, I don't except you to be, but I want to be honest with where I stand."

"All I am saying is I need time to figure out what is happening here. I want you and I am not saying for only one night, yet forever seems like a long time," Nikki said softly.

"It is, so before you come to my bed, Nikki, you need to be okay with being mine for that long." His voice was low, yet in no way did it lack conviction.

A blush lit up her face, warming her from head to toe, turning her thoughts to lust. He sensed it, he savored it, and he vowed he would taste it on her lips, along with her declaration to be his.

They returned to his house just as the sun was coming up. He stole a few heated kisses with her outside her bedroom door. He couldn't get enough of her long, open-mouthed sighs yet he wouldn't take her, not yet.

He left her with the taste of his mouth and a burning need for his touch.

NIKKI

Sleep didn't come easily, even though she was beyond tired. The sexual frustration Sebastian had raised in her kept her awake for a few hours more. When she did fall asleep, her dreams were of him.

The next time she opened her eyes, the clock said one pm. Groaning, she forced herself to get up. He had done an excellent job at making her forget her fear, but in turn had left her facing a huge inner conflict.

He had no plans to finish what they had started, not till she was ready to face the insane idea of being his — and only his — for the rest of her life. Part of her was ready to give him that, yet common sense stepped in to say, *Are you crazy*?

So *was* she crazy? Perhaps, some of the time, but this was asking a bit much way too soon.

She got up with the sound reasoning she didn't need to be in his bed. If and when she felt she was willing to be all his would be fine with her. So what if he was hot, sexy and charming? No need for her to lose her head!

Turned out, when someone was as fine as Sebastian, it was really, really hard not to lose your mind. And the man had no shame! When he finally came downstairs, where she was eating a bowl of raisin bran, he wore nothing but his boxers.

Freshly showered with water droplets still glistening on his hard pecs was just mean! Nikki licked her lips like a woman dying of thirst as he moved around making his own meal.

"I hate you," Nikki whispered when he stretched up to grab a cup.

He smirked as if he'd heard her, but she knew that wasn't possible. Still, it was unfair how tempting he was.

This kept up all day, and when she finally found her bed again, he was on her mind.

The next morning dawned with only six more days till Christmas. The body of the missing girl had yet to be found, the media had learned about Angie and Nikki had gone on location to report, much to Sebastian's annoyance.

"No more reports, Nikki," he growled as he drove her back to his house.

"I have a job to do," she reminded him.

"Which I said was fine till it became risky. It's no longer safe for you to be in the public eye."

"Fine! Keep me locked up!" she snapped.

"I will!" he answered, with just as much anger.

The next two days they nearly killed each other with their tempers. Nikki was on edge because her body felt like hell. One minute she was hot, the next she was cold before once more being fine.

Sebastian was dealing with stress at work. None of the leads were panning out. Lisa's body hadn't turned up and it was now four days till Christmas. He seemed to be lacking sleep: always keeping watch over Nikki was making him crazy too.

The next day he informed her they were going to a hotel for a change of scenery. Nikki didn't say much, but secretly she was glad. If she had to spend another day in this place with Officer Grumpy she would lose it!

The hotel he chose was one of Boston's largest. On the top floor they could see the city twinkling below. He was called into work not more than thirty minutes after checking in, and he posted four rather than the usual two officers outside the door before leaving her.

Nikki was glad for some alone time, even if four men did stand just outside the room. She turned on the TV, ordered room service and settled in for a relaxing night. After a few hours of pointless reality shows, she went to test out the large Jacuzzi bathtub.

The hot water and jets soothed her into a boneless heap of flesh. Any stress she had been carrying in her neck and shoulders melted away. Her eyes where growing heavy. Keeping them open soon became impossible so she gave in, letting them close.

Hovering somewhere between wakefulness and sleep, Nikki felt a funny kind of dizziness wash over her. Her first thought was, it was due to the heat from the Jacuzzi, yet even though her mind was telling her body to move, nothing happened. Panic started to set in when it became clear something was utterly wrong.

Terrified of drowning, Nikki fought with all her willpower to open her eyes, but when she was finally able to accomplish this the panic turned to downright, chilling fright! A man stood at the end of the tub. His hair was sandy-blond, his eyes the purest blue, and while everything seemed to paint angelic features, the curve of his lips and the glint in his eyes screamed evil!

"Hello, Nikki England." His words, soft and almost musical, filled her senses, yet he hadn't opened his mouth. "Did you think you could avoid me? The Collector? You can't, you know… escape your death." His lips broke into a full smile. "Now, I know you can't speak at the moment, but just think your response and I'll hear you."

Nikki did think. She thought, *Are you the Silent Night Killer?* She also thought, I *am not going to be ticked off your list!*

"I hate that nickname! I am not killing to symbolize anything. I simply take twelve souls during this time of year because it gives me the most bang for my kill. You could say it makes a soul all that more valuable and I just happen to like women."

He winked at her.

"And you will be mine, Nikki, even if someone else has tried claiming you. I will take your soul before you join the ranks of the undead!" His voice echoed in her head.

He was gone, and so was the hold on her body. Gasping, she sat up. Stumbling out of the Jacuzzi, she didn't bother to grab a towel. She raced to the living room, leaving a trail of water behind her.

It took her a moment of frantic searching for her cell so she could call Sebastian before she realized he was already there. Standing in front of the hotel room door, looking at her with two raised eyebrows.

Nikki didn't think twice about being wet or naked, she darted right into his arms before she started to sob.

"What's wrong? What happened?" he asked, as he half pulled, half carried her to the living room sofa.

"I saw him, he isn't human, Sebastian! He isn't human!" Her words jumbled together in a mix of gasps.

"Who isn't human?" he asked softly.

"The Silent Night Killer! He hates the name, by the way. He says he is a collector — the Collector of souls!"

"You talked to him? How? When?" Sebastian demanded, his voice sharp.

"He just showed up in the bathroom! I couldn't move, I couldn't even speak! I heard him talk in my head, his mouth didn't move!"

She started to bawl again, much to her embarrassment.

Nikki felt Sebastian's arms go stiff. He seemed to stop breathing for what felt like minutes, even though she knew that wasn't possible. Then he gently pushed her away to look at her face. He asked her to tell him everything.

She managed to stop crying long enough to tell him every detail of what had happened. When she was finished, he looked a little ashy as he pinched the bridge of his nose between his fingers.

"You're right. He is not human, he is a demon."

"A demon?" she wondered out loud.

"Nikki, there are more than just humans in our world. There are lots of creature that call this planet home: demons, witches and even... our kind," he said as he looked into eyes.

"Humans?"

"No, I'm not... human."

"But you just said 'our kind'... and I'm human."

"Nikki, your human days are numbered." His voice cracked just a little with his words.

"What are you saying, Sebastian? Because it sounds like you're saying I'm going to turn into something... but turn into what?"

She was backing up as she spoke, till she was at the end of the sofa.

"You don't remember because I took your memories, but we met before what you thought was our first encounter. You witnessed me kill someone — he deserved death, but you didn't know that — and you saw me for what I really was. I followed you home, charmed my way into your house and then I bit you."

When he finally raised his face, the pupils of his eyes were glowing a deep red.

"Vampire! You're a vampire!" Nikki couldn't stop herself from jumping up, even as her common sense told her outrunning a vampire wasn't doable!

"Yes, and you will be too," he reminded her gently, as if it was no big deal.

"Because you bit me?" she clarified.

"Actually, a bite won't change you. I drained your blood till you were nearly dead, and then I fed you my blood."

"Holy shit! You killed me! You made me a member of the Undead Club! That is what creepy blonde demon meant when he was muttering about me being undead and claimed. So you claimed me, didn't you?" Nikki demanded.

"I did kill you, but only to have you reborn as something stronger. And no, I haven't claimed you! I have been trying my damnedest to stop that from happening. But you haven't made it easy, I assure you!" He was growling at her now.

"Oh, I'm so sorry if I made claiming me so flipping hard, Mr. Vampire. How exactly would you like me to make it easier for you?!" Nikki asked icily.

"Simple. Stop trying to seduce me!" he retorted.

All the anger went out of her on hearing this. Then Nikki blushed as she realized how getting claimed really happened. He had to sleep with her first to work the magic vampire sex claim, or whatever!

"Oh. I didn't know," she muttered softly.

"Yes. This is why I wouldn't let myself make love to you, Nikki, because you would become mine forever."

Nikki slumped down to the floor as his words from the other night started to make more sense. He wanted her to be sure this was forever because it was literally! Her mind was racing with vampire things, being a target for a serial killer slash demon and the feelings she had for a real flesh and blood vampire!

"Nikki?"

She met his gaze but couldn't think of a single word to say! What did a soon-to-be vampire say to her maker anyway? *Thanks for the bite? You're damn hot so biting me doesn't count against you? I will forever be twenty-seven... thanks?*

Logic told her she should be more pissed, like, *Hey asshole, you killed me! No, I don't want to spend forever with a blood-drinking monster!* Yet neither of those was what she felt. True, it was overwhelming, but how could any sane human take on board being a vampire without it overloading their brain? They couldn't! Nikki knew she could either look at this as a curse or a gift: the choice was hers.

Once she had worked this out for herself, she got to her feet, still buttass naked, and crocked a finger at Sebastian. To give him his due, he looked at her with a worried gaze before cocking his head to the side.

"Listen vampire, I have dealt with a lot of insane shit in the last half an hour, and I only need one thing from you."

"What?" His tone was slightly apprehensive.

"You. I want you to claim me." She whispered the last part.

"No! You haven't had enough time to process all of this."

"I have, and while I can't fathom with my simple human mind what being a vampire is really going to mean, I can understand what my heart is telling me. It wants you, Sebastian, vampire or not. And I am not saying it's love, but forever will be long enough to figure it out... if I'm not killed by a demon first!" Nikki ended with shrug.

"You're crazy, Nikki, you know this, right? You're being hunted by a demon, have learned you will soon be a vampire, and yet you still want only one thing... sex!" He laughed.

Sebastian was standing in front of her in a blink of an eye, his hands cupping her face while dark eyes searched hers. The emotions she saw running across his face pulled at her own, making a thick, intense shield around them.

"Nikki, when I take you to my bed, when I fill you, those lost memories will resurface and you might end up hating me. But it will be too late... you will be mine."

His words broke on her lips as his mouth moved slowly over them.

"I won't," she promised.

"This is what worries me. You have no idea how intense a vampire claim is. No idea," he whispered in her ear.

Nikki closed her eyes, enjoying the feeling of his lips so close to her neck. He was nibbling on her earlobe. She wasn't thinking about vampires or claims, not with Sebastian intent on making love to her. Not when she knew there would be no stopping this time.

She fumbled slightly with the buttons on his shirt. Once she managed to slide it off him, her eyes took in those hard muscles along his chest all the way down to the dip of his hips. Sebastian didn't have any slack anywhere!

He didn't give her nearly enough time to admire what he had to offer. He swung her up in his arms, making his way toward the bed and dropping her on it before covering her naked body with his own.

"Say the words, Nikki!" he growled in her ear.

"Forever… forever," she chanted relentlessly into his shoulder.

Sebastian's hands moved to cup her bottom, pressing her moist opening to his hard erection. His lips drank from hers, pulling soft moans and sighs from them, before moving to the hollow of her throat. This was the first she felt of his fangs.

Maybe it should have made her panic, even if just a little, but all it did was intensify her desire. He moved his lips lower to graze around the valley between her breasts before he took a nipple in his mouth, turning it into a hard little peak.

You're beautiful... beautiful," he droned repeatedly against her skin, his mouth teasing her senses as his hands urged her closer to a brink she couldn't fully explain.

Nikki fought to get her chance to touch and taste him. Using his thick unruly hair as a weapon, she pulled till he gave up his devotion to her breast. Quickly she sealed her lips to his, enacting a duel of tongues, each trying to outdo the other.

Clearly he was the master for she had to pull away, gasping for breath, while he merely smiled with a wicked tilt to his lips. The look in his dark eyes was hot enough to set fire to every Christmas tree in Boston!

"Playtime's over, Nikki."

Her insides tighten with those sultry words as Sebastian took hold of her ankle, tugging till her bottom rested on his knees, the look of white hot lust clear in the glow of his eyes.

Now she felt a jolt of panic as he once more poised above her, hard, well-defined arms holding his weight as he looked into her eyes. Pausing, perhaps to give her a chance to change her mind? Well, she wouldn't! Instead she met his gaze with a passionate one of her own.

He spread her legs now, moving himself into position to claim her. He brought his mouth to hers, kissing her senseless once more. Making her forget whatever fears were now resting in her soul. Trailing hot wet kisses to her neck as his hardness pressed into her softness, making her moan.

Nikki's eyes flew open as his fangs sunk once more into her tender flesh, but the all-too-real jolt of fear passed as he pushed past her opening, filling her completely. He moved slowly, making her hips respond of their own will.

Her eyes once more fluttered shut as he moved in and out of her body, faster with each thrust. He no longer had his fangs in her throat — his mouth was drinking her cries as he rode her. It was a high unlike anything she had ever felt before. Sex was never like this!

Nikki knew her nails were dug in too deeply on his back and that her love bites where drawing blood of their own. Still, she couldn't rein in the feeling of power and freedom which came with making love to Sebastian.

With a blur of movement, she found herself on his lap. He was still guiding her hips at a steady pace meeting with his thrust and he didn't even flinch when her nails sank deeper. A low approving grunt was all he gave her.

His lips stole another dozen or so kisses at her breast before moving to her shoulder where he once more bit her, tasting her, making her pleasure rise to a whole other level. Nikki knew she was close to losing control, to losing all her reasoning. She felt the build of her climax from a mile away.

Her scream echoed around the bedroom. Her arms gave out and she landed on his chest only to find herself once more below him as he entered her one last time, letting loose a cry of fulfillment all his own.

Leaning his forehead against hers, he placed a kiss to her temple before rolling off her. A faint beeping became clear as he moved around the room and sanity once more filled her head.

"What is that?" Nikki half yawned.

"The hotel room alarm."

"Someone is breaking in?" She didn't like the rush of dread the thought brought her.

"No, I think our... um, love-making set it off." He blushed ever so lightly.

"Oh," Nikki sighed sleepily.

"I'll be right back," he promised as he slipped out the door.

Nikki was close to blissful sleep when a flashback hit her like a jackhammer. Wincing, she set up, trying to catch her breath.

"Shit!" she muttered, still feeling the pain of the memory, and, like a sappy movie scene, all the events Sebastian had erased rushed back to her.

The pain of his bite, the fear of what she had seen. Even though she now knew the reason behind everything that had happened, the feelings of that night were strong and real. She didn't want forever and ever with Sebastian!

How could she want someone who had broken into her home, mind-fucked her and then had the balls to ensure she would forever be his? Sure, she didn't want to leave him — the feeling to stay and forgive him was strong. But, luckily for her, the feeling of hurt and betrayal was stronger!

Nikki didn't even finish putting her clothes on before an idea hit, making her blood turn to ice. The idea she had been thinking right before she had opened her door to Sebastian that night... What if he was the killer? He had found the house, he had been assigned to watch her and he had the ability to play mind games with people!

The more Nikki thought about it, the sicker she felt. As calmly as she could, she went into the bathroom and waited till she heard Sebastian come back to bed. Opening the door with what she hoped was a steady hand, she walked around the bed and to the door leading into the living room.

"Hey, are you okay?" Sebastian called out.

"Yep, getting water," she answered in a steady voice.

When he didn't say anything else, she sprinted to the door. Once she'd closed the door behind her and was in the hallway outside, she called Steven. He would be up.

"It's late," he grumbled into the phone.

"I know, but please pick me up at the Hilton downtown."

She didn't bother with the details. No one was going to believe her!

Standing in the lobby barefoot and jumpy as a junkie, she waited for the news van. When the white van with the blue station logo pulled up out front, she had never been more thankful for anything... ever!

"Drive!" she yelled at Steven as she opened the door and jumped in.

Shocked, to say the least, Steven looked at her and then at the large man charging at them from the lobby and stepped on the gas.

"Nikki, what the hell? Why are we running away from Officer Jamison?"

"Because I have good reason to think he is the Silent Night Killer, now drive!" Nikki ordered before dialing her mother's number. "Mom? Hey, guess what! I'm coming home after all! Yep, see you soon!"

Nikki hung up and her phone started to ring. She looked down to see it was Sebastian, and she hit deny.

"Your mom lives four hours away, Nikki! Either we are going to end up in jail for speeding away from Jamison or, if you're right, dead because sexy, eye-candy cop is the Silent Killer!" Steven muttered.

"I'm sorry, Steven, I truly am for getting you involved. You're going to have to stay at my mom's too... for a while." Nikki didn't want Sebastian to hunt him down for helping her.

"Oh God! Our boss is going to have a fit!"

"Look, does it matter if he has a fit? I don't think you want to end up naked and dead in a creepy shack, do you?" Nikki asked.

"Point taken," Steven agreed with a roll of his eyes.

"And my mom can't know about this, so for the time being you're my boyfriend. Got it? You and I are dating. I don't want my mom to freak out about me being stalked by a killer." Nikki gave Steven a long, hard look.

"Nikki, I am not sure your mother is going to buy that we are dating, seeing how at this moment I don't even like you. At all!" he glared.

"She will. She has to," Nikki warned.

The rest of the drive was done with no talking on Nikki's part, but that didn't stop Steven from complaining the whole trip.

Once Nikki and Steven stood outside her mother's front door, Nikki was fairly sure they hadn't been followed by her vampire.

Her mother was happy to see her, and while she kept giving Steven the once-over suspiciously, Nikki thought she believed their story of boyfriend and girlfriend. Even tucked into her own bed, hundreds of miles from Boston and Sebastian, the sense of doom hung over Nikki like a dense fog and sleep was hard to come by.

Sebastian

Standing in the snow outside the hotel in nothing but his sweat pants, Sebastian was gaining his share of looks. It didn't matter, however, not when Nikki was now out of his protection and possibly his claim. He always knew there was a chance this would be how it ended once she regained her memories from the night he had bitten her.

Still, he had hoped she would know by now he cared for her; that he would not let any harm come to her. Instead he felt her fear and confusion as she raced out the hotel door and into the night. He saw the van and knew Steven had picked her up.

If he had to guess, he would assume Nikki would head to her mother's. After all, this was where most children went to seek comfort from the world when things got bad, but surely Nikki wouldn't want to bring the demon to her mother. Yet she would have to go somewhere for money and clothes.

He called his partner and told him to have officers from here to Storm King on the lookout for the news van, assuming she was heading to her mother's, and to move the remaining women to a convent. The demon wouldn't be able to set foot in a place like that! Now here he stood, still staring off into the falling snow, wondering where the hell Nikki had ran off to and why.

Sure, the truth of what she felt was going to hit her hard, and he could understand this, but what he couldn't handle was her up and leaving so abruptly. He couldn't figure out why she was suddenly so fearful? Surely the whole vampire thing wasn't what had sent her fleeing? After all, she was only twenty-four hours from joining the ranks.

No, something else had sent her into the night, and he was damn sure going to find out what. His cell rang, bringing him out of his thoughts.

"You lost her." The voice was soft, clean in a way that sent his heart into a slower hum in his chest.

"Lost who?" Sebastian asked, playing into the killer's hands.

"Why, your prize! What else would have you standing out here in the winter barely dressed with the humans staring at you? You don't like attention… vampire." The last word he hissed.

"I don't crave it like you do, that's for sure, demon."

"Demon? What a naughty word. Worse than the name your blood-bags gave me… What was it again? Silent Night Killer? Truly horrid!" He purred now, his voice a mix of angelic and demonic rolled into one.

"You won't be getting away with your little games much longer. I know what you are now and I know how to send you back to where you crawled free from!" Sebastian snapped his cell closed in disgust as he made his way back inside the hotel.

The ringing of his phone followed him into the elevator and he answered once more, knowing the demon wasn't ready to end his taunts.

"You have some twisted sense of value, blood-drinker, if you think you are pure enough to handle the weapons it would take to send me back to my maker!" He laughed at this.

"I know what I am, and you're right: my kind is not much of a step up from yours, but a step up we are. I have been around for a while and I know a few tricks, body-jumper," Sebastian sneered.

It was true he couldn't cast the demon out himself — he wasn't unsullied enough for it— but he could show Nikki how to do it. If she would listen to him. One thing was clear at the moment: the demon didn't know where Nikki was. Being in a human body gave him limitations, and while a demon was strong, his host body brought weakness.

"Then let's see who wins this little soul-stealing game, shall we?" The line went dead.

Sebastian finished dressing quickly, then went back to the satiation. He wanted to look for Nikki and the clock was ticking down. The demon wasn't going to give up, not with his track record. Whatever he got for killing souls was too powerful to give up.

Sebastian couldn't leave it to chance, not when it meant Nikki's life was at stake. If she still wanted to run from him after she was safe from actual death, then she could. This didn't mean he wouldn't chase her, but in order for them to have this option she had to live long enough to change into a vampire!

Sebastian had done a background check on Nikki the night he had bitten her. He had learned a little about her life up to that point, including where her mother lived. He was busy trying to get the local police of Storm King to do a drive-by of Nikki's mother's house when his cell started to ring. He answered it, putting the local cop he was talking to onto hold.

"Hello, Officer Jamison," he said.

"Sebastian! Oh my God, I need your help! I killed Steven… I think I really did. Please come!" Nikki was sobbing into the phone.

"Nikki? Where are you?" he asked, as calm as he could manage.

"I'm thirty miles north of Storm King. Please, something is wrong with me!"

"I'll be there." He ended the call.

He could appear there faster than his car could drive, so he moved into the darkness of night, closed his eyes and thought of Nikki — of where she was. It was all he needed: a clear connection to her.

Soft rain and the taste of salt told him he'd been successful. She was kneeling on the asphalt near a blue Oldsmobile. On the ground was Steven, a nasty gash in his neck still seeping blood.

When Nikki looked up her eyes were wild and blood smeared her mouth and was running down her chin. Her hands were also covered in blood and lay limp in her lap. A rush of fear ran across her face as she looked at him.

"How...?" she began, looking at him

"It's a perk of being a vampire," he told her softly.

"Nikki, what happened?"

"We left my mom's. I couldn't bring... I couldn't let anything happen to her, so we just started to drive, trying to get as far away from Boston as possible, when out of the blue, I got this hunger. And next thing I know, I'm sinking my teeth into Steven's neck and drinking!" Nikki started to cry again

"Nikki, you're only hours from your change, this is why your urges are getting stronger. This is why you should have stayed and let me help you!" Sebastian told her.

"I couldn't stay after what I thought I knew. I thought you were *him*... that you killed all those girls. I don't know what is real anymore," she whispered.

"Yes, you do. You know me, Nikki. You can sense what I really am. Try," he pleaded with her.

Nikki looked up, her eyes shining like a rainy sky, half aqua, half grey, and he felt his heart squeeze. This was his mate! The realization of this hit him hard.

For what felt like a lifetime he sat across from her in the rain in the middle of nowhere with a dying man between them and everything he had ever wanted on the line. This was it. Was she really his?

"Sebastian, I… am yours." Those where the best three words he had ever heard.

"Nikki, we need to get help for Steven," Sebastian reminded her as he pulled out his phone.

Calling the local police back, he had them send an ambulance and he managed to wake Steven up long even to wipe the memory of Nikki's attack. Nikki wanted to be at the hospital when her friend woke up so they followed the ambulance there in the newsvan.

Sebastian didn't want to add another traumatic event to her list tonight, but Sebastian knew if he didn't give her the tools to end the demon's existence then she could end up six feet down for good. They waited long enough for them to learn that Steven was going to be just fine then he pulled her gently into the hallway.

"Nikki, the demon is hunting you, and you are the only one who can end his reign of terror over your city. I am going to teach you how to do this… then I am going to use you as bait."

He didn't like it but he had no other choice.

"Sebastian, just promise me one thing."

"Anything."

"We will win."

She poked her head round the door then took one more look at her friend and co-worker before turning and holding her hand out to Sebastian.

Fortunately, teaching someone how to kill a demon could be done in public. It wasn't going to draw attention to them. In fact, it would probably amaze people how easy it was. Well, easy as long as you could get the words out.

First thing you needed to kill a demon was a Bible. *Common sense to anyone with half a brain*, Sebastian thought, but surprisingly few could separate fiction and Hollywood from the truth. Besides the word of God, you needed only one more thing: to be human and to have not committed murder. There you had it: no crosses no daggers, no holy water. Nikki was finding this hard to buy as well.

"That's it? No sword of truth or crossbow that shoots wooden stakes?"

"Nothing of the sort, just the Bible. What's more powerful than the word of God to those who fear it and Him?" Sebastian asked.

"I get it. It makes sense, but I just thought it would be more... oh, what's the word... epic?" Nikki said, making a sweeping gesture with her hands.

"You are about to face a monster, Nikki, a serial killer that has stalked your city for years during the most festive month of the year, and you don't find this epic?"

Her eyes went wide as she thought about what she was going to do. A demon seemed so farfetched, but looking at him, as she had for years, as the Silent Night Killer gave her a new perspective on what she was about to face.

"It will all be over with." She exhaled the words.

"Yes," Sebastian confirmed.

"Will he fall for our trap?"

"He isn't going to back down, even if he assumes we are luring him in. He will come for you. Nikki. I'm not going to leave you alone for long: once he's there, I will be too. I need you to say the words 'I cast thee out, I send you back from whence you came'. Chant it over and over as many times as it takes... all right?" Sebastian said, gently placing his hands on her shoulders.

"And what will you be doing?"

"I'm going to keep the monster busy!"

NIKKI

There were only two hours until Christmas Eve, and either way she looked at it, Nikki was going to die. Only thing was, would it be a permanent death? Or a temporary one? She was hoping for the latter because if she faced this demon, Silent Night Killer — a monster whichever name she used — and lost, well it wasn't going to be a Merry Christmas!

How ironic to be facing a dilemma where death was the only outcome. Really, there was so much going on inside of her right now Nikki felt like she was close to losing her grip on sanity.

What she did have a firm grip on was an old, faded Bible. She was clutching it so hard her knuckles had gone white. Her heart was beating sporadically as her body prepared for becoming undead and her breathing was short and shallow. Fear ran up her spine and back down, making her a little woozy, or was that due to her pending change?

Shaking her head, she walked back and forth in front of her fireplace. This was her home — the one place she should feel safe — yet it might as well have been the most haunted place in America for the amount of anxiety she felt at the moment. Then again, waiting for a demon who had killed eighty or so people in the last three years would surely put the bravest of souls in a panic.

Sebastian had promised to show up when the demon did, but even knowing how quickly he could appear after traveling his way back to Boston, she worried he wouldn't be quick enough.

Nikki had just turned to resume her pacing when a movement in the dark corner of her living room caught her eye. The shadow cast him in darkness as he slowly moved toward her.

"I knew it wouldn't be long." His voice was so icky sweet it hurt her insides.

Nikki closed her eyes, recalling the phrase she had to repeat, and when she opened them she found herself just inches from the demon now. He looked much the same as when he had shown himself to her last time, but now he wasn't as pretty and perfect looking.

"I like it when they choke on their fear!" he gushed happily.

"I cast thee out, I send you back from whence you came." Nikki gasped. The words physically hurt to say!

The demon gasped too, stumbling back a few steps, before he came at her full force. She was in the middle of saying the phrase again but stopped halfway through when he rammed his shoulder into her chest, sending her flying toward the wall. Yet it wasn't the hardness of the wall she smashed into. No, it was a hardness of another kind — one that was quick to wrap two arms around her before twirling her behind him.

"Keep chanting!" he demanded.

So Nikki did. Standing behind Sebastian, she chanted the line over and over again. The demon didn't like it and he lunged at her over and over, except each time Sebastian was there to fend him off.

The demon suddenly threw his head back, letting out a screech like she had never heard before, so loud it echoed through her house in a horrible wail. It stunned her enough that she stopped chanting.

The demon used this break to jump Sebastian, his mouth opening to show rows of sharp teeth. This was definitely not the mouth of a human! The demon's teeth sank into Sebastian's neck. Blood splattered everywhere, some drops splashing onto Nikki.

"Nikki!" Sebastian choked.

Quickly she started up chanting again. The demon held onto Sebastian, though, for what felt like a lifetime before Sebastian finally twisted away, rolling and moaning toward the sofa. Nikki saw all the blood coming from his neck and she whimpered every so softly.

He shot her a look, one which clearly told her not to stop, so she chanted faster, now so fast the words seemed to be tripping over each other. The demon made it back to his feet and once more made a run at her.

Nikki had a choice to make: either let the demon knock her down and sink those wicked little teeth into her and end all hope of sending him back to hell, or she could suck up enough strength to test out her new vampire teeth in his neck.

Instead of letting him come to her, she met him halfway, surprising him enough she was able to knock him down first. Once she had him down, she sank her teeth into his neck. Nikki didn't like the taste of his blood but she held on like a mad dog.

Something was wrong. She was starting to feel woozy again so she sat up quickly, scrambling off his chest. She started to recite her lines again but it burned worse now and her vision was failing her!

This is it, she thought, as she spluttered out the words, each one more painful than the last, till she hit the floor. She saw the demon twitching on the ground next to Sebastian, who hadn't moved from where he'd fallen. Then her heart stopped beating and the world went dark.

Music brought Nikki out of the darkness. The tune of 'Jingle Bells' flooded her drowsy mind. The smell of cinnamon and vanilla floated in the air. She couldn't open her eyes, but at least her other senses seemed to be working.

This pleasant background was not what a new vamp would think to wake up to. Whatever happened to crypts and coffins? Nikki could feel she was laying on a comfortable mattress. She could hear running water, as if someone was showering, which pretty much told her she was in a house or hotel. Did Sebastian bring her back to his house? She didn't have a bed this nice back home. The unknown factor was making her crazy!

With renewed effort, she once more tried to open her eyelids, but it was as if they had turned into stone slabs. Yet, slowly, they did open, first as slits. Light pierced through her pupils, making her eyes clinch together again. Nikki fought with her body to get it to respond to her wishes.

When her eyes finally opened properly, what she saw made them fill with tears. Sebastian's room was full of Christmas! A small tree with glittering lights sat next to the window, which was trimmed in holly. The comforter was dark red atop crisp white sheets. 'Jingle Bells' faded away into 'Winter Wonderland'.

Winter wonderland was the perfect way to describe what Sebastian had done to his bedroom. Everything about it screamed "Happy Holidays!" The door to the bathroom swung open and a freshly-showered Sebastian in nothing but a pair of loose slacks filled the frame.

"Hi," he greeted her with a half-smile.

"Hi," she repeated, feeling strangely shy.

"Did you want to shower?" he asked her casually, as if she wasn't waking up as a vampire for the first time.

"Shower? Now?" she asked, a little dumbfounded.

"Yes, now. After all, your mother is going to be showing up in... oh, about an hour."

"My mother? You invited my mother over!" She forgot all about how hard it had been to just wake up this morning as she flew out of bed. She tangled in a sheet and hit the floor with a thud.

"Easy babe, you had a rough night," Sebastian reminded her.

"So, that really did happen?" She was starting to doubt it.

"If you are talking about killing a demon and transforming into a vampire, then yes, it really happened." He chuckled.

"He is dead then. And what about the others on his list?"

"The demon is gone, Alex Gail, the man whose body he inhabited, is behind bars and the other women are all safe as well. They stayed safe in the convent which I had them moved to once I knew what he was."

"But is that right? After all, Alex Gail wasn't exactly himself!" Nikki pointed out.

"True, but the demon would not have been able to take him over if he was a decent person to start with, Nikki. And while he doesn't recall killing any of the women besides the first, the fact he recalls that one means he did it. So rest assured, Dalen has it all under control," Sebastian promised her.

"Okay, so why are you being so blasé about it? I mean, I get its Christmas and I love what you did for me, this is amazing," she said, looking around the room to take it all in again. "But I just woke up as a vampire! What if I can't control my thirst? I could end up taking a bite out of my mom!"

Nikki didn't want to think about what could happen.

"I almost killed Steven, if you recall, and I can't risk anything like that again, I..."

Sebastian stopped her rant by sealing his lips over hers.

He kissed her till she forgot everything and was thinking about nothing but how good his hard chest felt smashed to hers. When he finally pulled away, she let out a moan of protest.

"We have lots of time for this, love, but what we don't have time for is getting ready for Christmas with your mom. I want your first Christmas as a member of the undead to be perfect."

Nikki sighed. She was a lucky girl! Sebastian was amazing and she got to spend forever with him! Still, she had so many question about this new life, Sebastian ended up having to drag her into the bathroom and disrobe her.

"Why did it burn when I spoke those words?" Nikki asked as Sebastian shoved her into the shower.

"You were killing a demon, Nikki, it's a serious thing. And the closer you got to becoming a vampire, the harder it became to say those words. Vampires can't send demons back to hell — we aren't pure enough."

"Oh," she muttered. "So, vampires are evil?"

"No, but we are not one of God's chosen people either."

"Why don't I feel blood-thirsty? Shouldn't I be starving for blood now that I am a vampire?" Nikki knew she was asking a lot of question but she had to know!

"The only time your blood lust gets out of hand is before your first change and when you put off feeding too long. We can go days without blood." Sebastian patiently explained.

"Really? Well, that is a little disappointing! I thought you had amazing control because you didn't attack me, and here I learn you weren't even pining after my blood!" Nikki snorted.

"For crying out loud, Nikki, this isn't some sappy teenage romance novel! We don't burn with thirst every second of our lives! Yes, we need it, but blood doesn't overpower our senses 24/7," Sebastian almost snapped.

"Excuse me, Mr. Expert Vampire, but I have nothing to base this on besides silly novels and movies!" Nikki retorted.

"Just so we are clear, we don't burn in the sun. We can go to church but we can't say prayers. A stake in the heart, if made out of silver, will kill us because, for some reason, silver doesn't mix well with our kind. A wooden one just hurts like hell! We have super hearing, strength and speed. But we can't turn into bats nor do we sleep in coffins. However, we do have heightened emotions and feelings."

He paused for a moment, long enough to open the shower door.

"Now, you have the basic of being a vampire, can you please put aside your curiosity long enough to enjoy the day I planned for you?"

Nikki nodded because she knew if she opened her mouth, she would end up asking him more questions which would only lead to more. After all, she made a living out of doing just that!

Sebastian ended up being full of surprises! Not only had he decked the house out but he somehow found time to buy her a beautiful dress. It was a sleeveless red silk dress which fit her perfectly. Along with that he had gotten her a black pearl wrap bracelet and a pair of Jimmy Choo black shoes.

He left her to get ready alone while he went downstairs to check on how dinner was coming along. Nikki wore her dark hair down and added only eye-shadow to finish her look. Staring in the full length mirror she had to admit she made for one hot vampire!

Nikki headed downstairs. Based on Sebastian's time frame, her mother would be here any moment now. She couldn't find Sebastian in the kitchen but the cook he had hired to make their meal told her he had gone upstairs to change.

The ding of the doorbell echoed through the house and Nikki felt her stomach tighten. She had never had her mother come to Boston for the holiday because she always went home. More pressing, she had never brought any guys home to meet her mother!

Her mother was dressed in a cute black sweater dress, her dark hair cut short in soft layers. The same aqua grey eyes looked her daughter over.

"You look stunning, honey!" her mother gushed, wrapping her in a warm hug.

Nikki didn't know if it was the relief at being able to enjoy the holidays or the fact, even as a vampire, she could enjoy her mother's company that brought tears to her eyes.

"Oh honey, don't cry! I don't want to miss up those pretty eyes!"

"It's okay, Mom, really, these are happy tears," Nikki promised her with another hug.

Nikki was leading her mom into the living room when Sebastian came down the stairs. He froze on the last step, his dark eyes roaming over every inch of her. She didn't take the time to notice his lingering stare because she was doing some looking of her own!

Dressed in an all-black tux with a red tie, Sebastian made for a dashing sight. His dark hair was swept back, showing off his face. And what a face it was! Her mother cleared her throat, bringing their attention to her.

"Alice, welcome to our home," Sebastian said, moving in to place a kiss on her cheek.

Nikki's mother blushed a little before breaking out in a smile. Yet she didn't seemed shocked that Sebastian wasn't Steven!

"Uh Mom, about Steven…"

Her mom didn't let her finish, however.

"Oh, I know all about that. Sebastian filled me in, so I know you two were doing some undercover reporting and Steven isn't really your boyfriend."

"Oh." What else could she say? *Sorry Mom, actually you're wrong. We were running away from a demon posing as a serial killer! Not likely!*

Sebastian was amazing at entertaining. Nikki knew her mother was having such a wonderful time, and when they opened gifts and she got a small golden key to his house, her mother broke out in her own tears of joy. The key was for her so she could feel free to come by whenever she liked. It was a touching gesture.

Nikki's gift was a white gold band with what she thought was a blood red ruby. However, Sebastian told her it was a rare red diamond.

"It's not a wedding ring, not yet, but I did want to show you I want a lifetime with you. This is a promise of what is to come." Sebastian slid it on her ring finger and placed a soft kiss to her hand.

Later in the evening, when the two women sat sipping hot cocoa, her mother leaned in and whispered, "I like this young man, Nikki. He loves you and I can't wait to start planning a wedding!" Her mother gave her a wink.

"I love him too, I just figured out how much today!"

Nikki was beaming ear to ear the whole night. Sebastian had promised a perfect Christmas and it was! Nikki hadn't been able to enjoy this holiday in long while, not with the Silent Night Killer making it a nightmare. But now he was gone and the city could once more look forward to a wonderful holiday season. No one else knew the killer was a demon, they didn't need to. What mattered was they knew he was no longer out there.

Nikki walked her mother outside a little after ten pm. Alice had a long drive home, and while they'd offered for her to stay the night, she wouldn't hear of imposing on them — not this time, anyway.

"Go enjoy the evening with your guy," her mother told her, shooing her back toward the house.

Nikki watched her mom pull out of the drive before she returned to the house. Walking on cloud nine totally made sense to her now! There was no way she could feel any happier or more content.

Sebastian was waiting for her in the hallway. Nikki didn't have to ask what he had in mind because the look in those eyes, so easy to read, spelled it out. He led her up the stairs and back to his bedroom.

With slow graceful movements, he shed his clothes until he stood there in nothing. His body danced with light from the Christmas tree. Moving in like a lion stalking prey, he closed the distance between them.

"Turn around," he told her.

Doing as he asked, she turned around and the sound of her zipper followed. The dress, which she could have pulled off over her head, fell to the floor in a whoosh of silk. Sebastian knew she could remove it herself; the point was, he wanted too.

Standing with her back to him in nothing but black undies and Jimmy Choos was a bit of turn on. He wrapped his arms around her waist before nuzzling his way to her neck where he placed a dozen soft kisses before turning her around.

They stopped to kiss a few more times before making it to the window sill where he once more turned her around, placing her hands on the cool stone. Her forehead rested on the window. His lips found her earlobe where he nibbled with his fangs, sending shivers down her spine.

"Nikki... I am yours," he whispered softly.

Those were the same words she had told him. She knew what he was saying: this was forever. He was sealing his promise.

His hands moved down her body, over her hips till he found what he was looking for. Sliding a finger inside her, his hot breath on the nape of her neck made her breathing spike. He teased her till she was wet.

With a tug, the thin panties ripped free. Moving his hands to her hips he slid inside. The feeling was overwhelmingly good. Nikki let out a whimper that steadily grew to louder moans as Sebastian moved inside her.

Each thrust became faster, and just before she broke apart, he pulled out, sliding her on top of him. Sitting on his lap he made good use of his mouth, using it to taste her, to swallow her cries. Her hands gripping onto his shoulders, she gave it her all.

His mouth broke from hers as his climax hit. He shouted her name as he poured himself into her. Nikki found her own release as she came, biting down hard on his shoulder. They sat this way for a while, simply enjoying their bodies being so entwined.

"Merry Christmas, Nikki," he whispered into her ear.

"Merry Christmas, Mr. Vampire," Nikki teased.

"I bet you didn't think your first Christmas as a member of the undead could be so good," he smiled as he carried her to the bed.

"No, I could never have pictured it would be like this." She smiled too as he rolled on top of her, his dark eyes pinning her with a soulful look. "I thought I would need time to say these words, but I love you, Sebastian."

She was happy with the look in his eyes at those words, such a pure refection of love.

"Nikki, I couldn't ask for a better Christmas gift than you and I love you." His lips once more found hers.

Wrapped up in her winter wonderland with the man of her dreams, being undead for Christmas really was the best gift a girl could ask for!

The End